Pirate Fish

written and photographed
by
Mia Coulton

A bag was on the table.

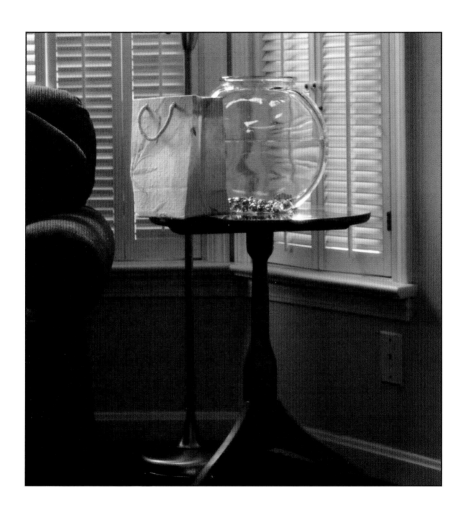

Inside the bag was
a treasure chest
with a lot of gold.

The treasure chest

and all the gold

went down

down

down.

Fish swam around

the treasure chest.

Fish was looking for gold.

Fish was a pirate fish.

Fish was behind

the treasure chest.

Fish was looking for gold.

Fish was a pirate fish.

"Arrr"